The Wish Wind

Wise wishes!

Peter Eyvindson

Peter Eyvindson

illustrated by

Wendy Wolsak

**PEMMICAN
PUBLICATIONS
INC.**

Design by Grandesign Ltd., Winnipeg, Manitoba.

Pemmican Publications Inc. gratefully acknowledges the assistance
to its publishing program by Manitoba Arts Council and Canada Council.

First Printing - October 1987   Second Printing - August 1988

PRINTED AND BOUND IN CANADA

Canadian Cataloguing in Publication Data

Eyvindson, Peter
   The wish wind

ISBN 0-921827-03-2

I. Wolsak, Wendy. II. Title.

PS8559.Y94W5 1987   jC813'.54   C87-098106-4
PZ7.E99Wi 1987

PEMMICAN
PUBLICATIONS
INC.

411 - 504 Main Street / Winnipeg, Manitoba / Canada R3B 1B8

For Konrad

"Come," whispered Wish Wind,
as he tossed a cascade of dancing
snowflakes at Boy. "Come, Boy,
and play."
But Boy did not come.

Teasing Boy,
Wish Wind joyfully caught up the
snowflakes in a happy whirlwind dance.
Still, Boy only sat there and scowled.

Playfully, Wish Wind whistled shrilly, as he twisted and darted his way up through the dark green boughs of Spruce.

But Boy would not listen to the Wish
Wind song. Instead, Boy only sat there
on his cold stump and grumbled.

"Winter! I hate it!" Boy complained bitterly. "I hate cold. I hate snow and ice. If it were springtime, things would be different. I wish it were Spring."

From up on high, Wish Wind heard Boy and came rushing down to whisper gently in Boy's ear, "Patience, Boy, and Spring will come."

"But I want Spring now," Boy whined. "I want
to feel the warmth of New Sun. I long to hear Meadowlark
and Robin sing. I want to see kites fly. Oh, how I wish
it were Spring."
Wish Wind blew softly. He knew what he must do.
He would miss Winter. But a wish had been made and it
must be granted. "Are you certain that is your wish?"
asked Wish Wind sadly.
"It is," Boy answered firmly. "I want Spring."

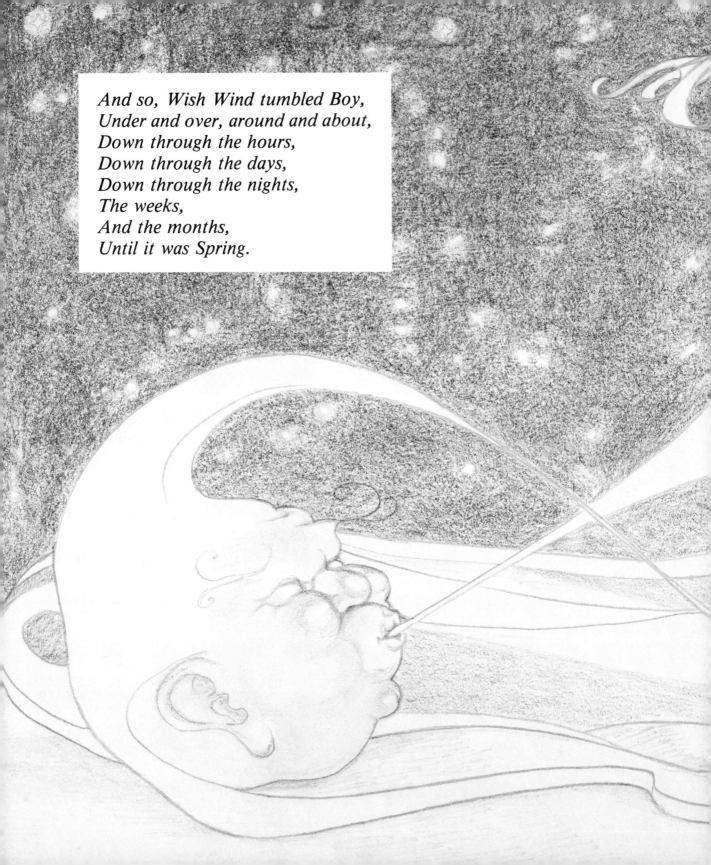

And so, Wish Wind tumbled Boy,
Under and over, around and about,
Down through the hours,
Down through the days,
Down through the nights,
The weeks,
And the months,
Until it was Spring.

For a time, Boy was happy.

He listened,
as Meadowlark and
Robin cheerfully sang
their songs for
Spring.

He lay on the grass and basked in the warmth
of New Sun. He watched as Wish Wind darted
about rustling the fresh, new, green
leaves of Poplar.

Boy laughed, as he watched Wish Wind
toss brightly coloured kites aimlessly across
the bright, blue sky.

But soon, Boy grew tired of Spring.
"Spring is boring."
Boy said wistfully,
"I wish, instead, it were Summer."

Brightly coloured kites
fell abruptly from the sky,
as Wish Wind stopped
in surprise. Once more,
he had heard a wish . . . a
wish that must
be granted.

"Boy," whispered Wish Wind sadly, "tell me you do not want the wish. Tell me, instead, that you need to enjoy the time that is now."

"No," whined Boy. "I want Summer. Spring water is too cool for swimming. I want Summer. I want Summer now. Grant me my wish, Wish Wind."

And so, Wish Wind sadly tumbled Boy,
Under and over, around and about,
Down through the hours,
Down through the days,
Down through the nights,
The weeks,
And the months,
Until it was Summer.

"Summertime!" yelled Boy excitedly,
as he splashed about happily.
"Now, Water is warm and inviting.
Now, I'll have fun!"

"Be careful, Boy," whispered Wish Wind, as he lapped Water into waves to make the shore sing. "Water is playful, but Water can also be deep and treacherous. Careful, Boy!"

But Boy only splashed his way through to deeper and deeper water.

"Careful, Boy,"
murmured Wish Wind.
"Beware of Water, Boy.
Please, be careful."

"Don't tell me to be careful," Boy shouted back angrily. "Leave me alone! If only I were older, then you would no longer tell me what to do. I wish I were old."

From far away, Boy thought he could hear
moaning and groaning, as suddenly, the sky grew black.
Angry slashes of lightning darted across the sky.

Suddenly, Wish Wind growled out his rage and tumbled Boy,
Under! Over! Around and about!
Wish Wind tumbled Boy,
Down through the days,
Down through the weeks,
The months,
And the years,
Until Boy was older . . .

. . . *much older.*
It was Autumn.
Old Man sat withered
and bent, dried up with age.
While Wish Wind snatched
and crackled dry leaves out of black
and gnarled Oak, the hollow cry of
the Loon mourned the death of Sun.

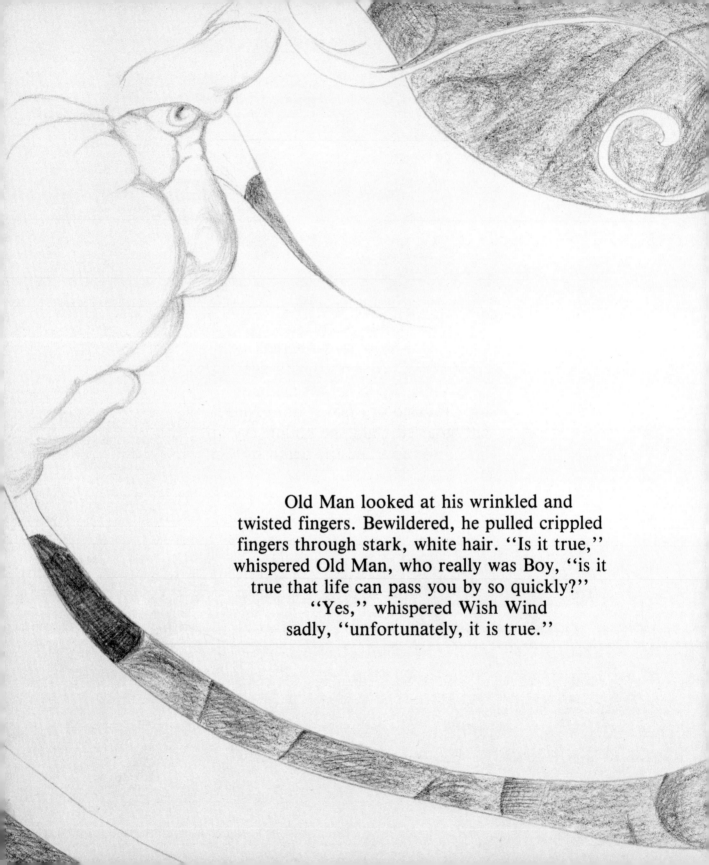

Old Man looked at his wrinkled and
twisted fingers. Bewildered, he pulled crippled
fingers through stark, white hair. "Is it true,"
whispered Old Man, who really was Boy, "is it
true that life can pass you by so quickly?"
"Yes," whispered Wish Wind
sadly, "unfortunately, it is true."

"I suppose that it is too late now,"
said Old Man gravely, "but if I had but
one last wish to make, I would wish only
that Boy be given the patience to enjoy
the time that is now."

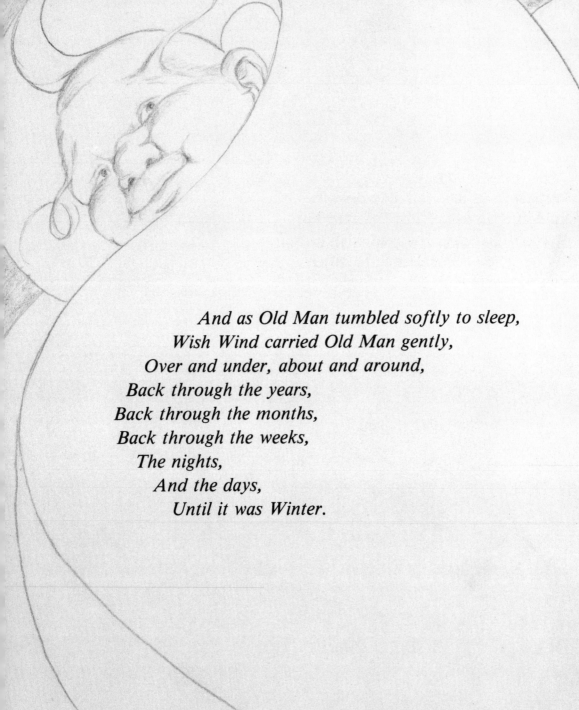

And as Old Man tumbled softly to sleep,
Wish Wind carried Old Man gently,
Over and under, about and around,
Back through the years,
Back through the months,
Back through the weeks,
The nights,
And the days,
Until it was Winter.

"Come,"
whispered Wish Wind,
as he tossed a cascade of dancing
snowflakes to waken Boy from his dream.
"Come. Come, Boy, and play."

And Boy did!